ADRENALINE RUSH

MOUNTAIN BIKING

ANNE-MARIE LAVAL

A+

Smart Apple Media

Published by Smart Apple Media,
an imprint of Black Rabbit Books
P.O. Box 3263, Mankato, Minnesota 56002
www.blackrabbitbooks.com

Printed in Printed in the United States
of America at Corporate Graphics,
North Mankato, Minnesota.

Published by arrangement with the
Watts Publishing Group LTD, London.

Library of Congress Cataloging-in-Publication Data

Laval, Anne-Marie.
Mountain biking / Anne-Marie Laval.
p. cm.—(Adrenaline rush)
Includes index.
Summary: "Explains the sport of Mountain
Biking (MTB), including the different types of
riding, such as cross-country, downhill, North
Shore, and marathon. Describes mountain bikes
and the features that make one bike better for
a riding style than another. Includes a list of
good places to ride, along with descriptions of
competitions and events"—Provided by publisher.
ISBN 978-1-59920-684-4 (library binding)
1. Mountain biking—Juvenile literature. I. Title.
GV1056.L39 2013
796.63--dc23
                              2011034976

PO1433
2-2012

9 8 7 6 5 4 3 2 1

Picture credits:
t–top, b–bottom, l–left, r–right, c–center
front cover Maxim Petrichuk/Dreamstime.com,
back cover Pink Tag/istockphoto.com, 1 Ljupco
Smokovski/Dreamstime.com, 4–5 Evelyn Pritchard,
5tr Brett Pelletier/Dreamstime.com, 5cl Evelyn
Pritchard, 6 Lukas Blazek/Dreamstime.com, 7t
courtesy of Jeff Archer, First Flight Bicycles, 7b
courtesy of twentynineinches.com, 8l Neil Harri-
son/Dreamstime.com, 9cr Maxim Petrichuk/
Dreamstime.com, 9br Pancaketom/Dreamstime.
com, 10–11 Ljupco Smokovski/Dreamstime.com,
11tr Evelyn Pritchard, 11bl Antonov Roman/
Shutterstock, 12 Maxim Petrichuk/Dreamstime.
com, 13tr Lane Erickson/Dreamstime.com, 13br
James F. Perry/Wikicommons, 14–15 Maxim
Petrichuk/Shutterstock.com, 15t Evelyn Pritchard,
16 2010 Getty Images, 17cr Maxim Petrichuk/
Dreamstime.com, 17br Jandrie Lombard/Dream-
stime.com, 18–19 Evelyn Pritchard, 19tr Neil
Harrison/Dreamstime.com, 20–21 Robert Coc-
quyt/ Dreamstime.com, 20bl Andrey Khrolenok/
Shutterstock.com, 22–23 Joe Hayhow/Shutter-
stock.com, 23tl Andrey Khrolenok/Shutterstock.
com, 23bl Jandrie Lombard/Dreamstime.com,
24–25 Torsten Lorenz/Shutterstock.com, 25tl
Shariff Che' Lah/Dreamstime.com, 25cr Maxim
Petrichuk/Dreamstime.com, 26–27 Maxim Petri-
chuk/Dreamstime.com, 27cr Maxim Petrichuk/
Dreamstime.com, 28–29 hipproductions/Shutter-
stock, 29br Doug Stacey/Shutterstock.com.

Words in **bold** are in the glossary on page 30.

CONTENTS

"Hit the dirt" is a mountain biking (MTB) phrase. It is the kind of thing you might say to your friend as you are about to start a ride together: "Let's hit the dirt." It also has another meaning—crashing!

This mountain bike racer is taking part in an event in hills above the sea in the Western Cape, South Africa.

The Most Popular Bike

What is it that makes MTB so popular? Partly it is because many people think the bikes look really cool. But mostly it is because it is just so much fun. With the right mountain bike you can:

• race your buddies down narrow trails through the woods.

• go **dirt jumping**.

• enter a cyclocross race.

• ride down a World Cup downhill course.

• go away for a weekend camping in the wilderness.

• ride to school, the mall, or a friend's house.

Mountain bikes really can do everything that can be done on two wheels.

World of Mountain Bikes

Show up at any **trailhead** in the world, and you will probably find mountain bikers getting ready to ride. Usually you get a warm welcome, especially if you give people a smile and say hello. MTB is a friendly sport, and most mountain bikers will help each other out with advice on where to ride, or help repair a flat tire or a mechanical problem.

MTB features cross-country races (above), long-distance events with overnight camping (left) and much more.

Top Three MTB Videos
MTB videos are often published in series; you can find many of them on Amazon.com. Here are three of the best:

- *Earthed—some of the most extreme downhill, ridden by some of the best riders in the world.*
- *New World Disorder (NWD)—focuses on freeride MTB, but there is lots of dirt jumping and street riding, too.*
- *West Coast Style—these videos show some basic techniques to get your skills up to par fast.*

People have been riding off-road for many years. It is only fairly recently, though, that bikes built especially for off-road riding were developed.

Special CX bikes have drop handlebars, like road bikes. You can enter most CX races on a mountain bike, too.

Cyclocross

Some people say that the earliest form of MTB is cyclocross (CX) racing, which started in the early 1900s. In a CX race, riders start at the same time, and follow a pre-set course. They ride as hard as they can for an hour, then finish the lap on which they are riding. The rider who has completed the most laps wins.

The Breezer Series II was one of the first ever custom-built mountain bikes.

Cruiser Racers

In the 1970s, a group of Californians started driving to the top of Mount Tamalpais in Marin County, and racing back down on their old **beach cruisers**. They kept breaking their bikes, so they started building better ones. That was the start of the modern mountain-bike business. Pretty soon, children everywhere were asking for Specialized Stumpjumpers or Marin Muirwood bikes.

Joe Breeze went to school at the foot of Mount Tamalpais in California, and was one of a group of friends who first started racing down its trails. Breeze built the first custom-built mountain bike, the Breezer Series I in 1977. Only nine were made, but Breeze kept building bikes. Today Breezer Bikes is still going strong.

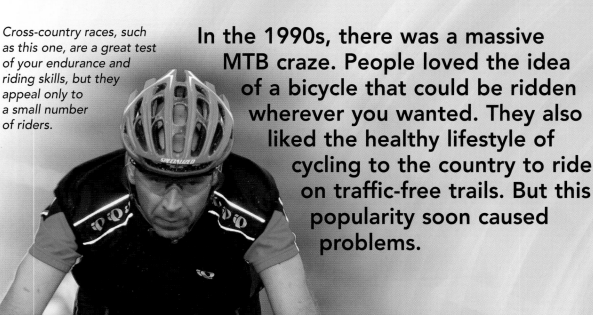

Cross-country races, such as this one, are a great test of your endurance and riding skills, but they appeal only to a small number of riders.

In the 1990s, there was a massive MTB craze. People loved the idea of a bicycle that could be ridden wherever you wanted. They also liked the healthy lifestyle of cycling to the country to ride on traffic-free trails. But this popularity soon caused problems.

Decline and Fall

Almost as quickly as it started, the MTB craze nearly died out. There were three big reasons for this:

• the rise of the BSO—BSO is short for "Bike-Shaped Object," a bike that looks like a mountain bike, but is cheaper than other MTBs and is not tough enough to be ridden hard. Anyone who bought one quickly quit MTB.

• competitions became focused on circuit races, similar to CX courses. Most people find this kind of riding boring to watch and to take part in.

• access to trails began to be restricted after complaints about out-of-control mountain bikers.

The Rebirth of MTB

In the early 2000s, mountain bikes became stronger, lighter, and more reliable. Manufacturers developed full-suspension machines that you could ride over almost any ground. Riders began to find new things to do on their bikes rather than just riding around in circles. With better bikes and an increase in the range of things you could do on a bike, MTB once again became popular.

All mountain bikers quickly learn how to fix a flat tire. Even with off-road tires, flats happen pretty often.

Some trails are closed to bikes because they are just for walkers or to stop soil erosion.

Trail Rules
Riders developed this set of rules so that all trail users could enoy riding:
- *ride only where it is allowed.*
- *leave no trace—no litter and no skid marks on fresh grass.*
- *control your bike.*
- *yeild to other trail users—never expect others to move aside for you.*
- *never scare animals.*

HELPFUL HINTS

Today there are many different types of mountain bikes, but the best bike for all-round use is still a hardtail. This is a bike with suspension forks at the front, but a rigid frame at the back. Hardtail bikes combine comfort and stiffness, and can be used for just about any kind of riding.

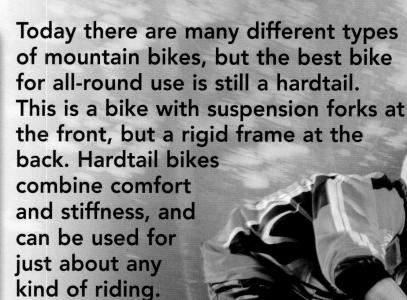

Gears
Bikes usually have 27 or 30 gears— enough to get you up or down just about any slope.

Forks
These move up and down to absorb shocks as the bike travels over rough or bumpy ground.

Tires
Knobby tires give grip and a bit of shock absorption.

Clipless pedals
They are called clipless, but they actually clip to the bottom of the shoes. These make controlling the bike easier.

Disc brakes
These are the same type of brakes that are used on cars and motorcycles, so they stop lightweight bikes extremely well.

Full-suspension bikes have to be ridden in a slightly different style from a hardtail. You have to keep your weight on the saddle for the rear suspension to work properly.

A modern hardtail bike, such as this one, can be used for almost any kind of riding, from downhill courses to cross-country, and even off-road touring.

Bike weight varies from about 20 lb. (9 kg) for a cross-country bike to 42 lb. (19 kg) for a downhill bike.

Suspension usually has about 4 in. (100 mm) **travel** on cross-country bikes, and up to 11.5 in. (300 mm) of travel on downhill bikes.

The size of the brake discs varies from 6.5 in. (160 mm) for cross-country to 8 in. (200 mm) in downhill. Bigger discs give the brakes better stopping power.

Full-Suspension Bikes

Some riders pick full-suspension bikes with shock absorbers on the front and rear. The tires rarely leave contact with the ground, so these bikes are fast and smooth to pedal. The suspension travel soaks up bumps, allowing riders to go more quickly over rough ground, especially downhill.

The disadvantages of full-suspension bikes are that they are usually heavier than hardtails, and there are more moving parts that can break.

Aside from a bike, you do not need a lot of equipment for MTB. The most important piece of gear is the one that protects you from serious damage—your helmet. Other pieces of equipment and clothing can make MTB life more comfortable.

Helmet
To work properly, this must be a good fit and strapped on tightly enough to stay on your head in an accident.

Padded shorts
These make riding for a long time more comfortable as they stop the saddle from rubbing against your skin. There are two main kinds: tight lycra ones, and baggy ones with a pad inside.

Glasses
These stop dirt from the wheels being flicked up into your eyes.

Padded gloves
Long distances or hard, bouncy downhill rides will be far less punishing on your hands with a good pair of padded gloves.

MTB shoes
The stiff soles transfer power to the cranks well, and grip on the soles helps if you have to put your foot down.

Other Equipment

Most mountain bikers like to carry water in a hydration pack (a backpack with a special container for water). A tube leads over the rider's shoulder, making it possible to drink with both hands on the handlebars—very handy if you are going over bumpy ground!

Many hydration packs have a bit of space for carrying equipment. Look inside a mountain biker's hydration pack, and you would probably find:

- a pump, spare inner tube, and repair patches, in case you get a flat tire.

- extra clothing, such as a warm top and a waterproof jacket.

- multi-tools, for making any emergency repairs.

MTB can be hard work, and you sweat out lots of fluids, so it is important to keep taking little sips of water.

Born in Dijon, France, Anne-Caro, as she is known, is one of the best mountain bikers ever. She has been world downhill champion 12 times, and has won the year-long World Cup four times. Anne-Caro has also won world championships at dual slalom four times, 4X twice, and BMX three times. She won the first-ever BMX Olympic gold medal at the Beijing Olympics in 2008.

ANNE-CAROLINE CHAUSSON

Cross-country riding is the kind of MTB most people first experience. A good cross-country ride usually has a bit of everything: some smooth trails through beautiful countryside, narrow paths through woods and undergrowth, bumpy downhills, and a bit of climbing—some riders *like* going uphill!

Cross-Country Bikes

The bikes used for cross-country are usually a bit lighter than other mountain bikes. The riders probably will not be doing jumps or hitting big rocks, so the bikes do not have to be as strong as downhill bikes. When riding uphill, though, having less weight in the frame and wheels can make the difference between making it to the top and having to get off and push.

During a race, the first rider to the top of the hill has a nice, clear run for the rest of the course.

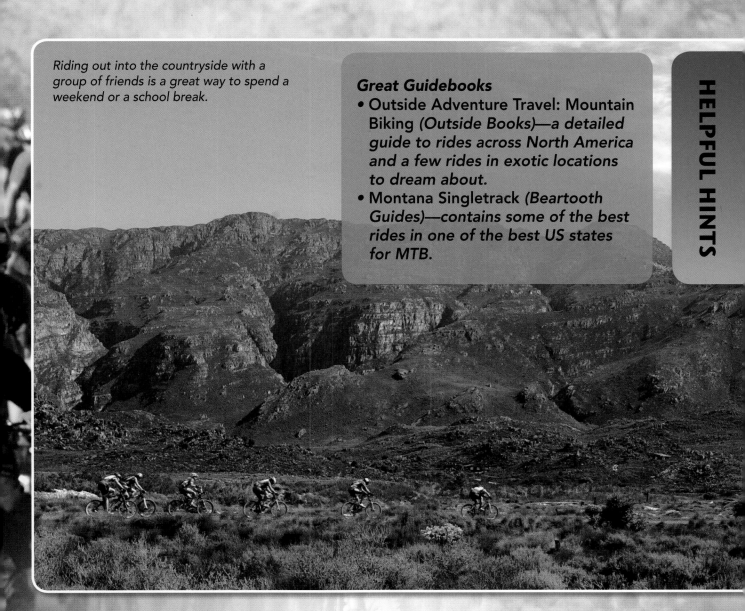

Riding out into the countryside with a group of friends is a great way to spend a weekend or a school break.

Great Guidebooks
- Outside Adventure Travel: Mountain Biking *(Outside Books)*—a detailed guide to rides across North America and a few rides in exotic locations to dream about.
- Montana Singletrack *(Beartooth Guides)*—contains some of the best rides in one of the best US states for MTB.

Singletrack Heaven

There is one kind of riding all mountain bikers love— singletrack. Singletrack gets it name from the fact that the trails are only wide enough for a single bike at a time to pass along them. Singletracks can run through all kinds of landscape, from rocky slopes to fields and flowery hillsides.

Many riders prefer singletracks that go through woods. Swooping through gaps between the trees is like racing in your own personal slalom contest. Hearing your friend's bike rattling along behind just encourages you to pedal that much harder.

In cross-country racing, the riders pedal around a circuit a set number of times, and the first rider across the finish line wins. The courses range from undemanding, flat routes that can be covered at high speed to tricky technical challenges that demand a lot of bike-handling skill.

Local Races

In the past, small, local cross-country races took place most weekends. Today, cross-country racing is less popular. It is sometimes possible to find a local MTB race, but more often riders take part in a cyclocross race (see page 6).

Riders test out the course for the cross-country MTB race at the 2012 Olympics.

Olympic Racers

Cross-country riding is currently the only way for mountain bikers to get to the Olympics. Cross-country first appeared in the Olympics in 1996 at the Atlanta Games.

Hadleigh Park in Essex is the home of MTB at the London Olympics. The course is different from other Olympic courses because it is on open hillside rather than in a wooded area. An open hillside is exciting for spectators, but it makes racing more difficult because it is harder to get away from pursuers if they can see how far ahead you are.

Even with 30 gears, sometimes you just have to get off and push!

Julien Absalon comes from the Vosges region of France. The area's wooded hills are perfect for cross-country riding. Absalon dominated cross-country racing between 2004 and 2008. He won Olympic gold in Athens (2004) and Beijing (2008), and won the MTB world championship every year from 2004 to 2007.

JULIEN ABSALON

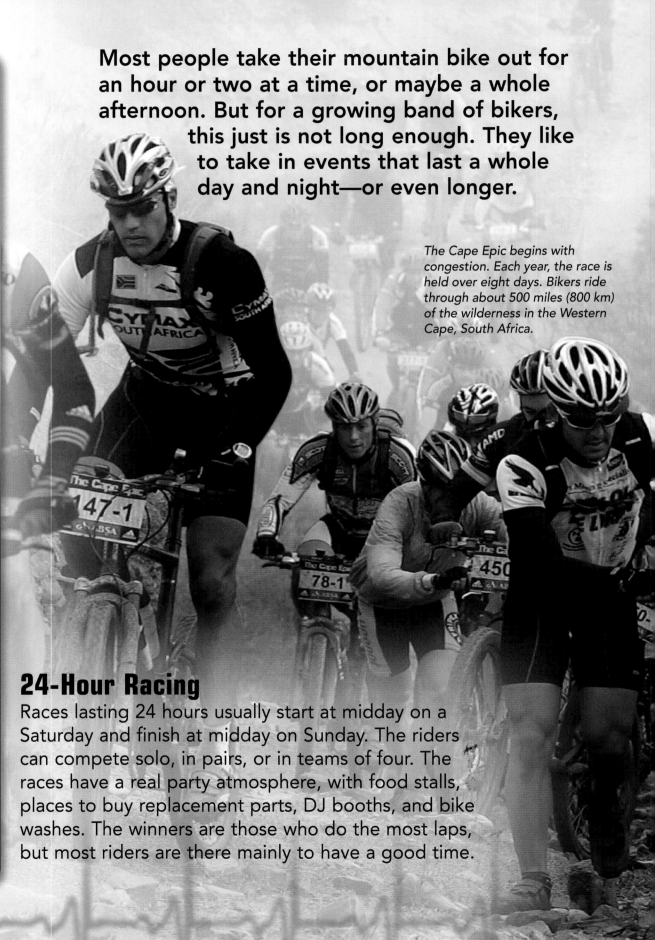

Most people take their mountain bike out for an hour or two at a time, or maybe a whole afternoon. But for a growing band of bikers, this just is not long enough. They like to take in events that last a whole day and night—or even longer.

The Cape Epic begins with congestion. Each year, the race is held over eight days. Bikers ride through about 500 miles (800 km) of the wilderness in the Western Cape, South Africa.

24-Hour Racing

Races lasting 24 hours usually start at midday on a Saturday and finish at midday on Sunday. The riders can compete solo, in pairs, or in teams of four. The races have a real party atmosphere, with food stalls, places to buy replacement parts, DJ booths, and bike washes. The winners are those who do the most laps, but most riders are there mainly to have a good time.

Long-Distance Endurance

For real long-distance riding fans, there are mountain bike races that take days to finish. These are usually solo rides, covering hundreds of miles. Sometimes, the racers have to carry all their gear with them in **panniers** or a **trailer**. In most long-distance races, though, a **support team** carries camping gear and spare clothes, leaving the rider free to go as fast as possible.

Top Three Endurance Races
- *Great Divide Race—an annual race down the spine of North America, from Canada to Mexico.*
- *Trans-Wales—a week-long race across Wales, with the riders following specially designed routes each day.*
- *Trans-Rockies—racers ride across the beautiful Canadian landscape in a week.*

IN ACTION

19

One of the spiritual homes of MTB is the North Shore Mountains of Vancouver, in Canada, an area that is filled with old forests. Here, mosses hang down from the trees and thick undergrowth deadens the sound, making it a magical place to ride.

A ladder ride over marshy ground on the North Shore.

Ladder Riders

The wet weather of the North Shore means that in places, boggy soil can swallow a bike up to its wheel **hubs**. Elsewhere, streams have cut deep chasms into the hillsides. To get over these obstacles, riders started building "**ladders**." Ladders are raised wooden paths to ride on.

This custom-built ladder track offers an extreme challenge to a rider's skills.

Extreme Skills

The demands of ladder riding meant that the riders quickly became experts at bike handling. Every year, they tackled harder and harder routes. Today, North Shore riding includes jumps, riding down near-vertical rock faces, and balance skills such as hopping a bike around a 90 degree bend on a ladder 30 feet (10 m) above the ground.

Top North Shore Video

North Shore History X—Todd "Digger" Fiander is considered one of the fathers of North Shore trail making. He's captured hours of footage of riders on his trails. Get a glimpse of all the thrills and spills that are North Shore riding in his movie.

If you are a fan of snowboarding, you will probably know all about boardercross. It is a thrills-and-spills race between four snowboarders, racing side-by-side down a course of jumps and sharp turns. Four-cross, which is usually written "4X," is a mountain-bike version of the same thing.

Dual Slalom and the Birth of 4X

Before 4X, there was a similar event called dual slalom. In this, two riders raced down parallel courses, with the first to finish the winner. 4X grew out of dual slalom, but instead of racing down four parallel courses, the riders all race down the same one. The course features jumps, banked turns known as **berms**, and other obstacles to test the riders.

One of MTB's key cornering skills is to always look ahead of where you want to go, rather than at the ground under your front wheel.

4X Contests

Contests start with every rider doing a timed run. The fastest half of the riders move on to the knockout stages. In knockouts, four riders leave the starting gates at the same time. They ride the course side-by-side, with the first one or two riders going through to the next round. After each round, the field is reduced by at least half, so the competition is fast and furious. There are always plenty of spectator-pleasing crashes, as racers desperately try to grab one of the top places.

Either this rider is way ahead—or he crashed and is dead last!

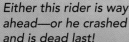

Australia's Jared Graves is one of the world's top 4X riders. He won the season-long World Cup competition in 2009 and 2010, and was also world champion in 2009 and 2010. Graves is also a top BMX rider, having come second in the 2008 World Cup and sixth at the 2008 Beijing Olympics. In his spare time, he takes part in top-level downhill races as well.

Most bikers start riding downhill by trying to get down their favorite route just a little bit faster than the last time (and just a little bit faster than their friends). But watch out—the challenge of getting down a slope as fast as you can is **addictive**.

Heavy Metal Riders

Downhill racing is the heavy metal of MTB—not everyone likes it, but you can't ignore it. The top riders are among a tiny number of people who can control a bike at speeds of 60 mph (100 kph), avoiding roots, rocks, and trees as they go. Very few riders have reflexes good enough, and even fewer are able to beat the fear of a crash.

Downhill bikes have to be very strong to absorb big hits!

24

Urban Downhill
When you think of MTB, you probably think of the countryside. Some downhill races, though, take place in cities. The riders rattle down steps, cross bridges, jump over roads, and career down concrete slopes.

Urban downhills have taken place in (among other cities):
- *Lisbon, Portugal*
- *Sarajevo, Bosnia*
- *Edinburgh, Scotland*
- *Cagliari, Sardinia*

Downhill Courses

Most downhill courses combine sections of track where the riders can go full speed with more technical challenges. It is often possible to ride around obstacles, but this is usually slower. This means the most skilled riders are able to set the fastest times.

Downhill Bikes and Equipment

Downhill bikes look almost like motocross bikes without engines. Because they travel downhill only, the bikes have to be tough, which makes them heavy. Downhill racers wear full body armor to protect themselves in a crash. A rider's chest, neck, shoulders, elbows, hips, and knees are all covered by hard armor. Racers also wear protective gloves, **full-face** helmets, and goggles.

Downhill racing is real crowd pleaser, as the riders rattle down tricky routes at high speed.

There are lots of good things about MTB. Most of all, it is fun and it keeps you fit. There is even evidence that regular exercise can improve your grades at school! MTB can also be dangerous—riders have been badly injured, or even killed, in accidents. So it pays to make your riding as safe as possible.

Top Tips for Riding Safe

Making a few simple checks every time you ride, and following some simple guidelines, can help to make MTB as safe as possible:

- equipment—always wear a helmet and other safety gear if you are doing extreme riding.

- check your bike before every ride— make sure the wheels are securely attached, the brakes work, and the handlebars and saddle are secure.

- know how to fall—if you do come off your bike, relax and try to roll or slide away, instead of slamming into the ground, a tree, or a rock.

Riding alone is never a good idea, and when riding in a group make sure everyone sticks together. Always ride at the pace of the slowest person, so no one falls behind.

Riding Rules

MTB is popular, and sometimes the trails get busy. Riders have developed a few guidelines to make things flow smoothly:

• try not to stop on a narrow or steep section of trail, where other riders will be forced to stop behind you.

• let faster riders pass (as soon as there is a safe place to stop) if you can hear them catching up behind.

• if you catch up to someone, do not shout at or harass them. It will make them nervous (and probably slower). Wait for them to let you pass.

• do not push too hard—never be pushed into trying something you are worried about, such as a big jump or a steep downhill. Fear makes your body tense up, which makes it unlikely that you will succeed.

• never follow someone else's **line**—just because there are tire tracks going along a trail, it does not mean you can follow at full speed. The riders in front might be better riders than you—or they might be wrapped around a tree just around the corner.

Right now, this rider is wondering whether taking part in a race over snow was such a good idea after all.

There are tens of thousands of great places to go riding. Wherever there is countryside, you will find people riding across it on mountain bikes. But where would you go riding if you won so much money that you could fly anywhere you wanted in a private jet? Here are a few ideas:

Marin County, California

You would have to take a trip to the place where MTB as we know it began—Marin County, and in particular Mount Tamalpais. The area has everything from long downhills to day-long cross-country rides.

Durango, Colorado

Durango is where the first mountain-bike world championships was held. It has just about every kind of riding, from downhills to cross-country trails.

Snowy Mountains, Australia

In winter, you can find some of Australia's best ski runs in the Snowy Mountains, but in summer, the area is great for MTB. In particular, the area around Mount Beauty, which is sometimes called Australia's mountain-bike capital, is worth a visit.

Riders cross the Alps. In the summer, the region is so popular with bikers that there are companies that do package trips especially for mountain bikers.

Chamonix, France

The Chamonix Valley is great for all kinds of extreme sports, especially MTB. Ski lifts carry you and your bike high up into the mountains, and you can spend all day zig-zagging your way down.

Åre, Sweden

Åre (pronounced "ore-uh") is mostly about **lift-assisted** downhill and freeride trails, and there is not much cross-country riding here.

Afan Forest Park, Wales

Some amazingly designed trails wind up and down the slopes of this valley. The singletrack through the forests is really exciting, and the tricky sections of Whytes Level and the Wall challenge even the best riders.

7stanes, Scotland

Not one, but eight MTB areas, showing off the best of Scotland's trails. At one of the areas, Innerleithen, ordinary riders can attempt the challenge of the UK's only World Cup downhill course.

A rider is put to the test at the Downhill World Cup in Scotland.

addictive
describes something that is hard to stop once you have started.

beach cruisers
old-fashioned single-speed bikes with big tires and wide handlebars.

berms
turns that are banked up, or raised, on one side.

dirt jumping
activity shared between mountain bikers and BMXers, where the riders jump off dirt ramps.

freeride MTB
a type of MTB where there is no set course. Riders make their way down the trail on the most creative line possible. Freeriding tests riders' style, control, and speed.

full-face
describes a helmet that protects the rider's chin and jaw as well as the head.

hubs
middle part of a wheel that allows the wheel to spin around.

ladders
raised paths made out of wooden poles and planks that allow riders to cross boggy ground.

lift-assisted
using a ski lift to go uphill.

line
route or direction riders go along the trail.

panniers
bags for carrying gear attached to the back of a bike on either side of the rear wheel.

support team
person or group of people who provide a rider with help during a race.

trailer
a wheeled cart towed behind a bike.

trailhead
place where a mountain-bike trail begins.

travel
amount of movement a bike's suspension has.

Competitions

World Cup
The International Cycling Union (UCI) World Cup is a season-long set of races, and awards the best rider over the course of the whole year. Events are held around the world. Go to www.uci.ch and click on "Mountain Bike" to get the latest rankings.

World Championships
The UCI also holds an annual one-off competition to crown the best rider. This champion may or may not be the same winner of the World Cup.

The Olympic Games
Cross-country MTB events have been featured at the Olympics since 1996. Go to www.olympic.org/mountain-bike to get information about the sport, equipment, and history.

Online Magazines

www.nsmb.com
A Canadian online magazine of the North Shore Mountain Bike group, with good articles of riders, equipment and news, plus an excellent videos section where you can watch clips of some amazing riding.

www.imbikemag.com
The International Mountain Bike Magazine has a range of articles about equipment, technique, places to ride, and much more.

www.singletrackworld.com
Online version of a print magazine, this site has a good range of articles, plus a forum where you can contact other riders for advice about technique, equipment, places to ride, and just about anything else to do with MTB.

INDEX